THE LAST TIME I SAW HARRIS

Frank Remkiewicz

THE LAST TIME I SAW HARRIS

Lothrop, Lee & Shepard Books   *New York*

For Sylvia

First Edition   1   2   3   4   5   6   7   8   9   10

Library of Congress Cataloging in Publication Data
Remkiewicz, Frank. The last time I saw Harris / by Frank Remkiewicz.
p.   cm.   Summary: When a fierce windstorm blows away his clever parrot Harris, Edmund is inconsolable and goes with the family chauffeur on a long search through town and country. ISBN 0-688-10291-3.—ISBN 0-688-10292-1 (lib. bdg.) [1. Parrots—Fiction.]   I. Title.   PZ7.R2835Las 1991 [E]—dc20
90-40263 CIP AC

Edmund's best friend was Harris.

Edmund taught Harris many things. Most of all they enjoyed playing color flash cards.

The harder Edmund tapped, the more excited Harris became. He knew red, orange, yellow, green, and blue. "When I teach him purple, he will know the whole color wheel," boasted Edmund.

Mama was delighted. "Perhaps he will become a great professor," she declared.

"I doubt it," said Papa. "He'll probably just keep eating birdseed and learn a few more words."

One day tragedy struck when a fierce windstorm sucked Harris out the parlor window.

Grief stricken, Edmund would neither eat nor leave his bed.

Each day Mama rented a new parrot from a talent agency.

Alas, none of them were skilled at playing color flash cards. Edmund grew pale and thin.

Papa summoned the chauffeur. "Higgins," he said, "take the car and find Harris. He'll be the only parrot that knows the entire color wheel except for purple."

"Very good, sir," said Higgins.

Hearing this, Edmund leaped from his bed. He gobbled a bowl of
clear broth and an almond croissant stuffed with avocado, grabbed his
flash cards, bounded into the car, and drove off with Higgins.

They searched in large cities.

And in undeveloped countrysides.

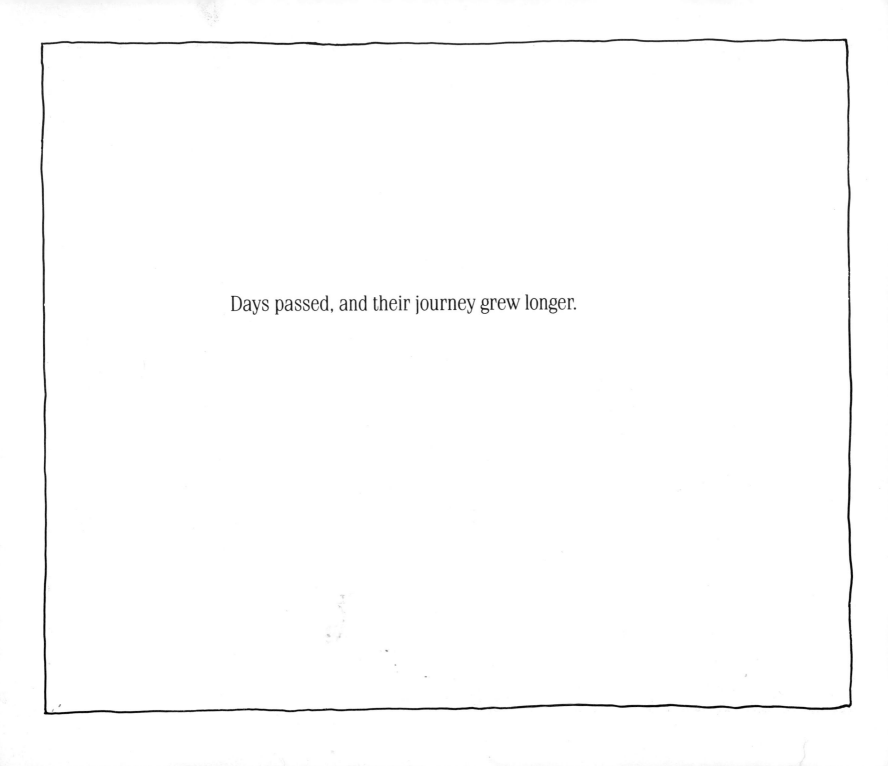

Days passed, and their journey grew longer.

Driving while showing flash cards proved difficult, and at times
Higgins lightly dented various parts of the car.

He always dutifully replaced them with similar panels from nearby auto wrecking yards.

At times it seemed they were on the brink of success.
But it was not to be.

Reluctantly, they began their long trip home.

They were almost home when Higgins slightly dented the trunk.
He replaced it with a lovely purple trunk from a nearby auto wrecking
yard, after which he and Edmund stopped for lunch under a large,
shapely tree.

Edmund's frustration was so great that he could barely eat. They had tried so hard and traveled so far. He pounded the trunk with his fist as hard as he could.

"PURPLE!" came a shriek from the tree high above them.
It was Harris!

The happy trio rode home while Harris recited the entire set of flash cards over and over.

What a joyous welcome! Mama searched for her guest list to plan a party, Edmund changed his clothes, and Higgins was allowed to take a nap.

THE END